# Caleb Johnson

## Mountain Man

## Snowbound

## Book Three

Charles Ray

D1372786

## 1.

The mule deer herd came slowly out of the thick woods near the far end of the box canyon, led by a large buck with six-point antlers which he wore proudly as he strolled leisurely at the front of his family of eight does, three of whom were already showing swelling of pregnancies that would deliver at the beginning of spring, and four young bucks not yet quite old enough or strong enough to challenge his dominance of the herd. The buck stopped ten yards from the tree line and sniffed the air cautiously, looking around in a wide circle to satisfy himself that it was safe for his family to graze on the lush grass on the broad plain that abutted the forest.

Caleb watched the herd from the blind he'd set up about a hundred yards from the trees, fortunately downwind of the deer.

He'd been tracking this particular herd for the better part of three days, watching their grazing habits from afar and mentally singling out the ones he would cull from the herd.

His first target was the larger of the four young bucks, almost as big as the leader of the herd, but with a less impressive rack, Caleb noticed that he often grazed near the leader, stopping to stare in a challenging manner until the old buck chased him to a more respectful distance. On one of his scouting forays, Caleb had seen the young buck approach one of the does, only to be butted away by the lead buck. This, he knew, was the prelude to a titanic struggle over leadership of the herd . . . unless the young challenger was removed from the herd.

As much as Caleb hated interfering in the unfolding of nature's order of things, he needed

1

to store up a good supply of meat for the winter. All signs pointed to the coming winter being colder and longer than had been the case for a while. There was a good chance, he thought, that he and his wife, Flora, could end up being snowed in for weeks at a time, unable to get to Bear Creek for supplies. So, he planned to have enough of the essentials to hold out. That included several trips to Bear Creek in the buckboard to get things like canned goods, flour, corn meal, salt, sugar, and other consumables that could be stored for later use. Flora had scoured the forests around their cabin for roots and herbs, which she dried and hung from the rafters. Now, he was putting the last piece in place, getting enough venison that could be cured and smoked and hung in the smoke house he'd attached to the barn, to see them through to spring.

He'd chosen the arrogant young buck as his first target. It looked to weigh in at nearly two hundred pounds, and being young, the meat wouldn't be as tough as the old buck's would. When he took it down, he knew the rest of the herd would flee into the forest, and it would be a day or more before they would dare return to the same pasture. They would return, though. Like most grass eaters, their brains were small in relation to their size, and they tended to forget danger
after a while. Their hunger would force them back to the same grazing spot. He would have to remove the carcass and clean up any blood stains as best he could. During the time he waited for the deer to come back, he could start skinning and dressing his kill.

With luck, he thought he should be able to take down two more of the young bucks, and be on his way home in a week to ten days. He'd already been out for a week, and he was missing home and his wife.

He missed her cooking. Missed sitting after supper and talking with her about her day. Most of all, though, he missed snuggling close to her under the blanket on cold nights, breathing in the sweet odor of her hair and feeling the warmth of her body.

Eyes closed for a few seconds, he pictured her as she'd been on the day that he left for the current hunting trip. He had swung out of bed before the sun came up and quietly made a pot of coffee, and fried some eggs and pork in the big iron skillet. The smell of the food and coffee had awakened her, but she stayed in bed, peering at him over the hem of the blanket that she'd pulled up over her nose.

"Mornin'," he said. "Want a cup of coffee?"

"No, I think I will sleep some more," she said. "I will go into Bear Creek to buy some new cloth for winter clothes."

"Be sure to take Dog with you."

She laughed.

"I do not think I could keep him from coming."

With that, she rolled over and soon he heard her snoring, a soft, bubbling sound that she made when she slept that, rather than annoying him, he found endearing.

He shook himself to clear thoughts of her from his mind.

*Gotta pay 'tention to what I'm here for. That deer ain't gon' shoot himself.*

The herd had settled in to grazing. Even the leader spent more time munching at the crunchy autumn grasses than looking around for danger.

Caleb raised his old buffalo rifle slowly, balancing it on a log he'd found in the woods. He took a steady aim on the buck he'd chosen, who fortunately was head-on to him, centering his front sight on a spot just to the left of the point where the left front foreleg joined the torso. He waited until the young buck raised its head to look around, and squeezed the trigger.

The bang of the old .50-90 Sharps was loud in the quiet of the valley, and the kick as the slug left the end of the barrel was hard against his shoulder. Accustomed to it, though, he kept his body steady and began swinging around toward the young buck nearest to his target, which had dropped to its front knees and was wheezing out its last before dropping dead to the ground. The sound of the rifle, accompanied by the smell of the blood spurting from the heart-shot young buck, had spooked the herd. The old buck's head went up and he looked directly at the spot where Caleb was busily trying to get a bead on the second young buck that had already began leaping toward the safety of the trees, followed closely by the rest of the herd, except for the leader. The old buck stood there looking intently in Caleb's direction. He could see out of the corner of his eye that the animal was as spooked as the rest, but was demonstrating its dominance.

Ten yards before the deer reached the trees, Caleb got a clear shot. Left side, just behind the top of the foreleg. The .50 caliber slug punched through and out the front of the deer's body, sending it cartwheeling to the ground.

The second shot was too much for the old buck. He turned, and with his black-tipped white tail flashing, fairly flew through the air in giant leaps to catch up with what was left of his herd.

4

Not, Caleb thought, that he would spend much time mourning the loss. Two less males to compete for dominance of the herd made the old male's life a whole lot easier.

"Shoot," Caleb muttered. "Not bad. Two in one go. 'Tween them two, 'n if I can git one more in a coupla days, there'll be more'n enough meat for the winter."

*Charles Ray*

2.

Flora Johnson flicked the reins, urging her pinto to pull the buckboard a bit faster. She hadn't bought much at the general store in Bear Creek, so the animal didn't have to strain. It broke into a canter, causing the old buckboard to shimmy and bounce on the dirt road that ran from the main road west from Bear Creek to the cabin in the hills she shared with the love of her life, Caleb.

She was anxious to get home. She looked west at the low, dark clouds that billowed around the tops of the distant peaks, hiding them from view. She'd seen a sky like this once before, when she was still a young girl. Such a sky in late November meant only one thing; bitterly cold wind and much snow was soon to follow.

The snow that year, she remembered, had fallen so heavily and so fast, that in less than an hour it was too deep to walk or even ride a horse through. Luckily, her village shaman, an old man of sixty winters, had recognized the signs and convinced the tribe's hunters to lay in meat, and the women to gather roots and herbs. For over a week, until the sun melted enough of the white blanket to allow them to move about, they had huddled in their tepees and eaten sparingly to make their food supply last.

She and Caleb had a good supply of just about everything at their cabin, and he was in the foothills now hunting mule deer to cure in the smokehouse attached to their barn, so they would be fine should the snows come like that again. She worried, though, about Caleb, out there somewhere, wondering if he could read the weather signs as she could, and would know that he should be heading toward home quickly.

Huddling inside the dark purple cape she'd made from some special fabric she'd purchased at Bear Creek's only dry good shop, she shivered from the icy breeze that blew east from the snow-capped mountains that she couldn't see.

Up ahead of the buckboard, Dog was as he usually did, nosing about in the brush from one side of the road to the other, looking for small animals to chase.

"Dog," she called. "Come here and sit up on the buckboard beside me."

Dog stopped and cocked his head at her. She knew that he was confused, because she seldom let him ride in the buckboard. But, for some reason, she felt the need to have him close.

"Come on, Dog. Do you not prefer to ride?"

Seeming to understand her, and realize that she was actually inviting him to sit next to her, Dog loped toward the buckboard and, in a leap almost made it onto the seat. His front legs hooked over the side, and scrambling with his hind legs, he managed to lever himself up, where he jumped onto the seat beside her, his tongue hanging out of the side of his mouth.

"You like it up here, do you?"

"Woof!" he responded.

"I will take that as a yes."

Dog leaned against her body. She could feel the warmth of his body and the vibrations as his tail thumped against the buckboard seat. It comforted her and almost took her mind off the worry she felt about Caleb somewhere up there in the foothills. She wondered if he was paying attention to the sky, and if he would understand that a really bad snowstorm was coming.

Not for the first time, she found herself wishing that she'd gone with him, or that he'd decided they could get the meat they needed from the general store in Bear Creek. But she knew he would never have done that. If she'd suggested it, he would've said, "Why should I pay the general store so much money for meat I can git with a couple slugs from my buffalo rifle? 'Sides, I don' like the way the cut 'n dress the meat. Them folks in town don' how to smoke or cure it right. Naw, I'll go git my own."

That was what she liked about him, but at the same time it frustrated her. He was his own man. Beholden to no one, dependent upon no one. He walked his own path, disdainful for those who moved in herds. In many ways he was like the grizzly bear, preferring to be off by himself to the company of what he called a bunch of squawking magpies in a town. She, he'd said on more than one occasion, was the only human companionship he needed.

She missed him so much her heart hurt.

*Charles Ray*

## 3.

It took Caleb the rest of the day, and well past midday of the next day to get the two deer's gutted and skinned. He'd been especially careful in taking the hides off. They were nice and thick, a sign of the coming winter, and once they were properly tanned, would fetch a nice price. He thought, he might keep one to make a jacket for Flora. It would look good on her.

After finishing that arduous task, he dug a hole and buried the entrails of the two deer, and then hung the skinned carcasses from the branches of a big tree near the lean-to he'd constructed from branches and pine straw in a little hollow in a tree-covered hill not far from the forest into which the deer herd had fled. Not far from the lean-to was a makeshift corral he'd constructed from limbs and branches of trees, in which the three horses munched away at the oats he'd scooped into a trough he'd carved out of a small dry log he'd found nearby. Another trough held water he'd gotten from the stream that flowed toward the mouth of the canyon about twenty yards from his lean-to.

He stood near his cook fire, letting the aroma of brewing coffee caress his nose, and stretched his shoulders and back, a bit sore from kneeling over the deer for so many hours.

It was only then that he glanced up at the sky. And, he didn't like what he saw.

Heavy, gray clouds seemed to be pressing down toward the earth below, obscuring his view of the mountains beyond the mouth of the canyon. The crowds billowed and rolled, and as he sniffed, he smelled a metallic odor in the air.

"Bad storm comin'," he muttered. "Guess I'll stop with two deer, 'n start for home tomorrow mornin'."

After checking on the three horses, and making sure nothing had tampered with the two deer carcasses, he set about gathering firewood. He'd felt the sting of a cold breeze against his face and realized that the temperature was about to take a nose dive into freezing territory, and soon from the force of the wind. He would build a fire that would burn for most of the night . . . he hoped, and keep him relatively warm.

When he had a good fire going, he started preparing his evening meal, which consisted of slabs of pork, beans, and biscuits that Flora had baked for him and bundled up in a large piece of muslin. They had become as hard as rocks, so he put them in a pan which set near the bubbling beans to allow the steam to soften them. While the pork was sizzling and the beans were bubbling, he started a pot of coffee, tossing in a couple of dried chicory roots for flavor. He sat back and enjoyed the mix of aromas from the coffee and food, and mentally mapped out the quickest route back to his cabin.

He took his time eating supper, topping it off with a second and third cup of coffee. He then constructed a wall of stones around his fire to bank it, and began shaking out his bedroll.

Looking up at the stars as he fell asleep was one of the things that he liked most about hunting, but overhead all he could see was black, as if the sky had been painted over. Icy zephyrs that tossed the embers from the fire around in the air were sure, he felt, to pick up strength during the night. Fortunately, the ground around his camp was moist, the evergreens were not dry and brittle, and the grass had absorbed moisture from the ground, so there was small danger of a fire starting. Just to be on the safe side, though, he piled more rocks atop his wall around the fire.

Just as he put the last rock in place, the wind began to pick up, making a low murmuring sound as it scraped over the and through the trees. He could feel the temperature dropping. Pulling his coat collar tight around his neck, he saw the white plume of vapor from his breathing. Even with the fire, he shivered from the sudden cold.

"Lord a mercy, ain't never felt this cold in November before," he muttered, his words muffled by the moaning sound of the frigid wind. "Better put a good amount of wood on this fire."

He felt good about piling up so much kindling before it turned too dark to see, and resolved to be heading for home at first light. In the dark, he heard the sound of the horses snorting and making low whinnying sounds, no doubt reacting to the sudden dip in temperature. They were sheltered against the worst of the wind, though, and would certainly huddle to share warmth. He found himself wishing he'd brought Dog along. The animal's warmth would have been a welcome addition to his blanket.

Despite knowing he needed his rest for the coming trip back home, he sat staring into the flickering flames, and drawing meaningless lines in the dirt near the fire for two hours. Finally, when he began to yawn, wrapping himself in two blankets and, using his saddle for a pillow, lying down facing the fire and drifting off to sleep.

His last thought before falling asleep was of Flora, wondering what she was doing, and if she missed snuggling up close to him under the blankets as much as he missed her at that moment.

He was sound asleep, and snoring when the first icy flakes of snow began to fall.

## 4.

When Caleb awoke the next morning, the fire had been reduced to a pile of glowing embers, emitting precious little warmth. He shivered even wrapped as he was in two wool blankets.

He opened his eyes, and blinked several times, wondering why he was unable to see his surroundings clearly. It was like looking into a blazing light. Only when he looked down at the ground upon which he lay did he realize what had happened.

The only dark area was the ground under his lean-to and around the fire.

Everything else was an even, pristine white.

It took his brain a few moments to process what he was seeing.

It had snowed while he slept.

Not a light dusting of snow either. Everywhere he looked, things were covered in white. Mounds of snow were piled against the trees up to mid-thigh, and in some places, drifts reached as high as his chin.

"Dang," he muttered. "Gittin' outta this valley ain't gon' be easy. I wonder if the openin' is blocked up."

He wasn't looking forward to taking h is horses through such deep snow, especially the pack animals. With full loads he couldn't push them too hard under such arduous conditions, and would be lucky to do five to six miles per day. With the mouth of the canyon fifteen miles from his camp site, he was looking at three to four days just to get out of the canyon, and depending on how much territory the blizzard had covered, more than a week to get home.

"Nothing for it but to do it," he said resignedly.

15

He got up and threw more kindling on the embers, blowing on them to get flames started. When the fire was burning the way he liked it, he first put coffee on, and sat for a while taking in the aroma. Then, he rummaged around in his pack and pulled out four pieces of pork and two eggs. He put the pork around the sides of his big iron skillet, and broke the two eggs in the center, letting them cook until the edges wee curling and brown before flipping them over. Once they were done to his satisfaction, he flipped them out onto his tin plate and put two biscuits in the grease that was now coating the entire skillet, letting the grease soak in along with the pork flavor. He took the biscuits out and placed them next to the eggs, and turned his attention back to the meat. He waited until it was brown and crispy before taking it out and adding it to his plate. He poured a cup of coffee, and sat with his back against the front pole of his lean-to and began eating.

He took his time with breakfast. Even though he'd planned on getting an early start, the deep snow would slow him so much it didn't much matter when he started, so he figured he might as well have one last leisurely meal before packing up.

Meal finished, skillet, plate, and spoon washed using snow, and packed away, he poured another cup of coffee, and sipped at it as he stowed the rest of his gear.

Gear packed and coffee cup empty, he looked around. The only thing left to do was empty the coffee pot and rinse it out with melted snow. After packing it and his cup away, he would then make sure the fire was completely extinguished.

Then would come the real work.

He would have to get the frozen deer carcasses down from where he'd hung them, and then prepare them to be slung on one of the pack horses. The rest of his gear, including the two deer hides, would go on the other pack horse. Only when he had everything packed and loaded would he then saddle Horse and begin what he knew would be the most arduous journey of his life.

The carcasses, completely frozen and coated with a layer of ice and snow, were hard to handle. They kept slipping from his grip, and the lack of flexibility made moving them difficult. He brushed off the snow, and chipped away the layer of ice with his knife, and then spent another thirty minutes dealing with Flora's pack horse's kicking and shying when he tried to secure the deer on her back. His pack horse was less of a challenge, but muscling the heavy bundles of gear and the two stiff deer hides onto her back left him sore and breathing hard.

He had to rest and flex his sore muscles before tackling putting a saddle on Horse, who nudged him gently with his muzzle as he tightened the cinch.

"Thanks, old fella," he said. "Reckon you know how much this old man's hurtin' right now. I sure hope you up to the ride ahead of us."

Horse snorted and whinnied loudly, the sound echoing in the valley and causing the other two horses to join in.

"Okay, y'all sound like you ready to go."

He grabbed the pack horses' reins and pulled himself into the saddle. With a gentle pressure of his knees, he got Horse moving toward the mouth of the canyon.

The wind, which had been mild since he'd awakened, began to pick up, whirling the snow into an almost impenetrable wall of white, making it a challenge for Caleb to stay on course for his intended destination. After several minutes of struggling to make sure he kept on a straight course, he gave up and stopped the horses. Taking Horse's reins, he moved off to the side toward what looked like a grove trees, and fortunately was, and moved into their shelter. Inside the grove, snow on the ground wasn't as thick, but the boughs above were heavily laden with snow that he knew could come pouring down at any moment. There was, though, nothing he could do about it. He hadn't realized how cold he was until he was in the shelter of the trees, and noticed that his arms were trembling. He could feel the cold seeping through his deerskin jacket.

He tied the three horses to a tree, relieved them of their burdens, and began scraping a clear spot to make a fire.

## 5.

He found just enough wood under the trees to get a fire going.

By the time the fire was big enough to send out any warmth, he was shaking all over, colder than he ever remembered being. Even though every limb ached, he pulled the deer carcasses and his gear close to add some more protection for the wind that managed to send its tendrils of stabbing cold in among the trees. Even the horses huddled close together, their heads low.

"Dang," he muttered. "Looks like it's gon' blow for a while. S'pose I might's well cook up some vittles."

Busying himself with preparing food, he was able to push some of the discomfort from the searing cold to the back of his mand, but never completely wipe it from his consciousness. As he prepared his own food, he wondered what he would do about the horses. The snow was too thick for them to be able to find grass, and he only had half a bag of oats left, about fifty pounds, which would last barely a day even if he put them on short rations.

When the coffee was ready, he poured a cup, and sipped at it while his beans boiled in the iron pot. The wind showed no signs of abating. He would have to plan on spending the night not all that far from his last camp. This meant he would have to construct some kind of shelter, and he would *have* to do something about food for the horses. Water, thankfully, was no problem. All he had to do was melt the snow.

He quickly ate his food, washing it down with a second cup of coffee, and began the process of constructing another lean-to. This one was

19

smaller and more rudimentary than the one he'd just abandoned, but it only had to keep him from being buried under any snow that the wind might shake from the tree branches. With that done, and his equipment and supplies safely tucked away underneath, he looked toward the horses.

The first order of business was to provide them with food. He walked to the tree. Noticing that the snow wasn't quite as deep under a nearby black oak. He found a fallen tree limb and began scraping it away until he'd exposed the wilted, bent grass beneath. It didn't look lush, but was at least thick, and under the circumstances, it was better than starving.

He scraped until he'd exposed an area about ten feet wide and ten feet long. Then, he untied the horses and re-tied them to a small tree at one side of the space. They immediately began munching at the grass.

Food for the horses taken care of, he began looking for a way to deal with the water situation. He tramped through the snow, mid-thigh deep in some places, until he found an old log that he was able to carve a hollow bowl shape in with his knife. He took that back and placed it where the horses could get to it, and filled it with snow. He knew that the snow would melt fairly quickly.

With his horses taken care of, he went back to the fire and poured another cup of coffee. Huddled in the lean-to to get out of the wind, he sipped and watched the wind-blown snowflakes melt as they came near the fire.

By the time his cup was empty, he realized that he had no idea what time it was. He couldn't see the sky, and the combination of snow and cloud cover meant that there were no shadows he could use. He had no idea if it was twilight or midafternoon. Everything was a uniform, gloomy shade of gray. It made him feel as dour as the weather.

He shook himself. He knew that letting himself get down was dangerous. Even at the best of times, the mountains could be a hazardous place, but with visibility restricted and trails obscured by the snow, it was downright deadly to let your mind wander.

He put his cup down, checked the fire, moved the coffee pot aside where it could stay warm but not become so hot the coffee left inside would boil off, and stood. He dusted off his trousers and took a deep breath.

Keeping the fire going until he was able to get on the trail again was important. He needed to gather enough firewood, a job not made easier by the restricted visibility and the snow-covered ground. Nevertheless, he would have to give it a try.

He began walking through the trees, careful putting his feet down to avoid stumbling on loose logs beneath the snow. A sprained or broken ankle under current conditions would be tantamount to a death sentence.

Fallen limbs suitable for firewood turned out to be easier to find than he'd anticipated. He nearly stumbled over the first one despite taking careful steps. It was a four-foot limb about half an inch thick with a forked end. He used it to scrape away the snow in front of him as he walked, and soon had an arm load of wood that he planned to place near the fire to dry out. With luck, he would be able to keep a fire going for a day or two, which he'd decided was as long as he would wait before striking out again for home. He would take his chances of getting disoriented in the snow if he had to. The danger was getting turned completely around, but that was offset by the fact that he was in a box canyon, and if he got on the wrong track would eventually encounter one of the walls which he could use to orient himself.

This thought was in his mind as he reached the edge of the clearing in which he'd made his camp.

He was just about to step into the clearing when he spotted the tawny body of a mountain lion, a big one, stalking across the clearing, heading for the horses who were downwind of it and had not picked up its scent.

His breath caught in his throat.

## 6.

Dog lay by the fireplace watching as Flora paced from one side of the room to the other, stopping occasionally to peer out the window with a worried look on her face.

She walked to the stove and filled a cup with coffee, walked to the table and put the cup down without taking a sip, and then went to the window where she used the sleeve of her deerskin jacket to wipe a circle in the condensation that had formed on the inside of the glass pane. Not that it did any good. All she could see was a swirling mass of white, snowflakes being whipped around by the wind.

The snow was so thick she couldn't even see the trees thirty yards from the front of the cabin. She stood there for a long time, her face so close to the glass her breath began to condense, blurring her view. Memories of the big snow of her childhood came flooding back. She wondered if this strange storm ranged that far west, and how the Shoshone were coping with it. Most of all, though, she wondered what Caleb was doing.

She knew that he was an experienced woodsman, and if anyone could survive such conditions, it would be him, but that didn't keep her from worrying. Worrying, and feeling guilty that she was safe and warm in the cabin that Caleb had built with his own hands, while he endured the freezing cold that she could sense on the other side of the cabin's thick log walls.

Hugging her jacket close around her body, she returned to the table. She picked up the cup and blew on the coffee although it wasn't needed, then took a sip.

Dog's tail thumped on the floor, and he looked up at her with his tongue lolling out.

"What is it, Dog?" she asked. "Are you hungry."

Dog made a 'whruf' sound and stood, stretching his body and yawning widely. He walked to her and rubbed his body against her leg.

"Yes, I think you are hungry." She walked to the pantry and looked inside. "Now, what should I make for us today?"

Dog looked at her with his head cocked to the left.

"It does not matter to you, does it? You eat whatever is put in your bowl."

"Woof," said Dog.

She continued to rummage around, looking at the labels on the various cans she had stacked neatly on the shelves. She reached for a can of beans.

"How does beans sound to you, Dog?"

"Woof?"

"Oh, you want meat as well, do you?"

"Woof, woof!"

She chuckled as she put the beans on the table and went to the 'cooler' Caleb had constructed. It was a chest set in the wall with a lid on the inside of the cabin, and three-fourth's of the chest outside. In the winter, the meat and other fresh foods in the part of the chest outside the house froze, while those in front, the part inside the cabin, stayed cold. Summers in their part of Colorado were seldom very hot, and since the cabin was surrounded by towering black oak trees, that part was always in shadow, and with wet straw wrapped in burlap surrounding it, things stayed relatively cool even then.

She smiled as she thought about her husband's creative mind. She took out a slab of pork from the back of the chest and took it to the counter next to the stove. With her sharpest knife and a lot of effort, she cut off four thick slices, and returned the main part of the pork to the cooler. Before closing it, she took out two large potatoes.

While the pork, which she'd arranged in the big cast iron skillet, began to sizzle as the heat thawed it out, she peeled and cubed the potatoes into a bowl. The aroma of the cooking meat aroused Dog, who left the fireplace and sat next to her staring up at the steam rising from the skillet with an expression of anticipation.

Flora looked down at him and laughed.

"I hope you will be this alert if someone attacks the cabin while Caleb is gone, Dog," she said.

He looked up at her and yawned.

Flora turned her attention back to her cooking. After turning the pork slices over and seeing that they had started turning brown, she dumped the diced potatoes in and began stirring them around in the grease

Dog's head went up and his tongue came out.

"Ha, so you know when the food is almost ready. You are a smart dog; do you know that?"

"Woof!"

"Of course, you do. Well, the potatoes are almost brown enough, so bet ready to eat."

"Woof," Dog said, and walked to the corner where she kept his food bowl. He took one look back at her and lapped water from the adjacent water bowl, then looked back at her.

"Do not look at me like that," she said. "I will bring you your food soon."

At the stern tone in her voice, he dropped to his haunches and sat staring into his empty food bowl. She smiled. It had amazed Caleb how quickly Dog had come under her spell, obeying her commands even when they were not spoken directly. A glance was all it took from her, for instance, to get him to go to his spot by the fireplace and lie down. It did not, however, surprise her. Even though she had never had a dog of her own, she had always had a way with animals; an ability to communicate with them in a way that no one else could, not even the most experienced hunters in her village.

When the pork and potatoes were done, she took a large wooden spoon and shoved some into a plate, then took the skillet to Dog's corner where she shoveled a slice of pork and a generous helping of potatoes into his bowl. He made a 'woof" sound that she knew was his way of saying, "Thank you, it's about time,' and shoved his snout into the food.

As Dog ate noisily, the only way he knew how to eat, she returned to the table, sat down, and pulled her plate across.

She began to idly eat, more picking at the food than actually consuming it. Now that she wasn't busy, thoughts of Caleb came back to the forefront of her mind. Her worry intensified.

"What are you doing, my husband?" she asked quietly. "Are you safe?"

## 7.

The mountain lion was big. Caleb estimated it weighed close to two hundred pounds. And, it looked desperately hungry, a dangerous situation at the best of times, but the lion was between him and his rifle and sidearm which he'd left under the blanket in the lean-to. He stood there with an arm full of kindling and only his knife at his waist.

The lion looked hungry. Not surprising given the weather. Food would be scarce. His horses, tied to a tree as they were, must have looked like a blue plate special at a restaurant.

He didn't cotton to taking on a full-grown mountain lion with nothing but an arm full of sticks and a knife, even one with a nine-inch blade, but he couldn't allow the cat to harm his horses. He crouched, keeping his eyes on the lion, and gently put the kindling on the snow. He picked out a sturdy looking limb, about four feet long and half an inch in diameter. He stood, and slowly and quietly, he began edging toward the cat.

Downwind of the cat, he didn't worry about it picking up his scent, even though, like most wild felines, it didn't have a well-developed sense of smell. What it did have, though, was highly-developed senses of sight and hearing, acquired over millions of years of hunting small prey in rough terrain. A mountain lion could hear the soft scuffling of a rabbit moving through scrub brush.

And, it was its sense of hearing that caused it to stop and turn to face Caleb.

He was fifty feet away at the time, so he knew that the cat could see him clearly, a dark figure against the white background. Smaller than the horses, he would be a prime target for the hungry feline, and had, he was sure, already diverted it from its original target.

Running away was out of the question, though. As fast as he was, and even with the deep snow cutting down the lion's fifty miles-per-hour running speed, it would also slow him, and it was unlikely he'd make it twenty yards before the cat overtook him. The animal could only maintain top speed for a few minutes, but in the snow, he would also be hampered. The last thing he wanted was a hungry mountain lion leaping at his exposed back.

He stood as tall as he could, and began waving the tree limb in the air.

"Hey, you big ugly old cat," he yelled at the top of his voice. "You better git your tail outta here 'fore I bash your head in."

Under normal conditions, his height advantage, and having made himself even bigger by waving his arms, and more intimidating by making loud noises, would have caused the mountain lion to decide to move on and hunt easier game. But the snow had driven most of its usual food underground or deeper into the forest, and it was hungry. Hungry enough to ignore the size disparity and the noise. It began stalking toward him, its tail waving from side to side, stretched out behind its body. Nearly six feet long, it was longer than Caleb was tall, and the look in its yellow eyes was that of a predator bent upon taking down its prey.

"Dagnabit, cat," Caleb said with a note of frustration. "I don' wanna hurt you, but if it comes down to me or you, I'll kill you. Now, g'on, git outta here."

In response, the cat picked up the pace, moving directly toward him now, its mouth open, revealing rows of razor-sharp teeth. The upper fangs were longer than Caleb's fingers.

He braced himself, his feet shoulder-width apart, and grasped the limb with both hands.

At ten yards, the cat started loping toward him, preparing to spring.

He waited. Holding his breath and watching it carefully.

Timing would be everything. If he was off by even a second, it would come down to a wrestling match between him and a hungry mountain lion that probably outweighed him by several pounds.

He continued to wait.

Then, the cat's muscled bunched up and its front paws left the ground. It was beginning its final leap.

When its hind paws left the ground, Caleb stepped nimbly to his right, swinging the limb in a wide arc with all his strength.

Unable to change direction in the air, the cat's sharp claws missed him by more than a foot. As its head passed him, Caleb brought the limb down onto its back, at the point where it joined the body, with enough force to smash it into the snow, where, stunned, it lay with its legs splayed out. Dazed, the cat shook its head.

"I'm sorry, old fella," Caleb said. "But you shoulda listened 'n run away."

He brought the limb down on the top of its head, hitting it so hard it split. It also opened up a gash in the cat's skull, weakening it enough to keep it from regaining its feet.

Caleb dropped the limb and pulled out his knife. Approaching the cat from the rear, he leaned over and grasped an ear and pulled its head back. He plunged the knife into the right side of its neck, just below the jaw and pulled outward, opening up a wide slit from which bright-red blood spurted in a thick cascade.

The cat made an attempt to growl, but all that came out was a gurgling sound and a geyser of blood. Caleb continued to make sawing motions with his knife until he'd almost severed the lion's head from its body. It gasped, spewing more blood, and went limp beneath him.

Caleb stood, wiping away the blood that had spattered on his face. He looked down at the lion with a sad expression.

He was not one to kill an animal except for its pelt, for food, or, as in this case, in self-defense. That he'd had no choice didn't make him feel any better about it. He took a deep breath.

"Now, I gotta git your carcass outta my camp so the smell of blood don' draw any of your friends, or scavengers," he said. "I sure wish you'd of found another place to go huntin' today."

After wiping the blade of his wife in the snow to remove the blood and bits of flesh, he put it back into its sheath. He grasped the lion's tail and began pulling it downhill from his camp, leaving a blotchy red trail in the snow.

Two hundred yards from his camp, he came to a small ravine that was only partially filled with snow. He dragged the lion to the edge and nudged it over with his boot. The carcass sank partway into the snow. Caleb found another large limb that had fallen from a tree, and used it to shovel snow into the ravine until the lion's body was covered. It would still be found by scavengers, but hopefully they would concentrate on it and not come near his camp.

Walking back to camp, he scuffed the snow to eliminate as much of the blood trail as possible.

The horses, still unaware of the drama that had unfolded just yards from where they stood, were nibbling at the few grass stalks that emerged from the snow. Caleb breathed a sigh of relief.

His fight with the lion had sapped most of the energy from him. He had just enough strength to retrieve the wood he'd dropped, and piled it near the fire.

He sat down and poured himself a cup of coffee.

With a sigh, he took a long sip of the hot brew.

Cradling the cup in his hands to absorb some of its warmth, he stared into the fire.

"It's gon' be a long night," he muttered. "Guess I'm gon' have to drink lots of coffee to stay awake. Can't afford to go to sleep now. Ain't no tellin' what else might be prowlin' 'round out there in the dark."

*Charles Ray*

## 8.

Caleb's head jerked up, and his hand twitched, spilling cold coffee on the leg of his trousers. The fire still burned, although it was burning low. The snow had stopped falling, and the wind was still. The sky was still overcast, but he could see a bright glow to the east in the mist, indicating that the sun was rising.

He realized that he'd fallen asleep sitting by the fire, and marveled that he'd not toppled over on his side, or worse, forward into the fire.

He yawned and reached for more wood to put on the fire, and began to prepare his breakfast.

While fresh coffee brewed and the food cooked, he looked again at the sky and determined that as soon as he finished eating, he would put the fire out, clean and stow his gear, strake camp and start for home. From the glow in the mist, he had a rough idea which way was east, and unless the weather changed, he would use that glow as a compass to guide him to the canyon mouth and back out to open country.

He took his time eating, and had three cups of coffee, figuring that due to his lack of sleep, he'd need it to keep from falling asleep in the saddle.

After finishing his breakfast, he carefully extinguished the fire and packed his gear. He left the lean-to for the next traveler who might come this way, and started the arduous task of putting the loads on the pack horses, starting with the deer carcasses, which, due to Flora's horse still objecting, was the most difficult task of the morning.

He carefully checked each horse's hooves, making sure they hadn't picked up any pebbles that could cause them to pull up lame, double checked the tie-downs of the loads, and then saddled Horse.

All the while, he kept an eye on the sky, looking for any signs of a change in the weather. Seeing none, he stood at Horse's side, rubbing absently mindedly at his shoulder.

"Well, old fella, we're gon' git started on what's likely to be the hardest trip we ever took." Horse snorted. "I know it's gon' be hard, 'n I'm askin' a lot of you. But I think you can do it. You gotta do it. Jest think 'bout bein' home in your warm stable, with me 'n Flora bringin' you oats every day, 'n makin' sure you got fresh water to drink."

Horse tossed his head and whinnied.

"That's the spirit," Caleb said. "I'm gon' be dependin' on you to set the pace for the other horses, you know. We ain't gon' push it too hard, but I'd like to be outta this dang canyon 'fore nightfall. You think you can do it?"

Horse tossed his head again, and pawed at the snow-covered ground.

"Thought you could."

He took the reins of the pack horses and mounted Horse, settling in the saddle to a comfortable position.

"Okay, old friend," he said. "Let's go home."

## 9.

Flora was pacing back and forth near the cabin's front door. Dog, lying in front of the fireplace, tracked her movements, his head swiveling right, then left, then right again. Sensitive to her moods, he sensed that she was distressed. He whined.

"I feel the same way, Dog," she said. "Caleb should be home by now. The snow stopped two days ago.

She stopped walking and stared down at the animal.

"I am worried."

Dog whined again.

"I do not know what to do, Dog."

Dog got up from the deerskin mat she'd put there for him to sleep on, and padded to her side. He put his cold nose against her hand, and whined.

"You are worried about him, too, aren't you?"

"Woof!"

Dog walked to the door and stood there, staring at it.

"He is not outside, Dog. I have looked through the window. There is nothing there but snow."

She went to the window, though, rubbed a circle, and looked again, her brow creasing in worry. Folding her arms under her breasts, she looked down at Dog.

"See, I told you he was not there."

Dog looked up at her, and she was sure she saw worry in his big brown eyes. She felt the sting of hot tears forming in her eyes. She shook herself and wiped them away.

"Come, let us eat." She strode across the floor to the kitchen. "I do not know about you, but I am hungry."

Dog followed her, his head hung low, and his tail trailing limply behind. That worried her even more. Dog was always wagging his tail. Even when he slept, the sound of his tail brushing across the floor often woke her in the middle of the night. She noticed that since Caleb left on his hunting trip, he wasn't wagging his tail as much anymore.

"What would you like to eat, Dog?"

She went to the cooler and took out a slab of pork, which she held up.

"Woof," said Dog. His tail wagged listlessly.

"Very well, then. Pork it is."

She took the slab to the work table, took out her largest, sharpest knife, and began sawing off slices from the partially-frozen slab. Dog's tail wagged with a little more animation. She smiled. He would probably become downcast again once he'd finished eating, but for the moment, his dog brain was focused on the meat she was carving.

When she had six slices, she took the remainder of the slab back to the cooler. From the pantry, she took a can of beans and a can of pears. The pears, of course, were not for Dog. Caleb had cautioned her against giving him sweets to avoid him getting worms. When she used the knife to open the beans, and poured them into a pot, his tail wagged even more.

She put the pot on the stove, followed by the meat which she'd put in a big iron skillet. The room was soon filled with the aroma of pork and beans. Dog's tongue lolled out of the side of his mouth. He sat back on his haunches with his eyes fixed on the stove.

While they were cooking, she opened the pears and poured them into a bowl, thinking that there was far too much for her to eat alone, which brought her mind back to Caleb. Oh, how she wished he was there, standing behind her, looking over her shoulder as she cooked. She wiped away more tears.

When the meat and beans were done, she put some of each in Dog's bowl, and put it aside to cool. If she gave it to him, he would immediately begin to eat, burning his mouth. When he saw his bowl on the table, he stood and walked to a spot just below where it sat, staring up as if he could make it move down to where he could get at it. One thing he did not do, because on the occasions when he did, it earned him a swat across the nose from Flora, was rear up and put his front paws on the table in an effort to reach the bowl.

"Just be patient, Dog. It will be cool enough to eat very soon."

"Woof!"

"You are as bad as Caleb, Dog. He, too, does not like to wait for his food."

She held a hand over the bowl, and decided that it was cool enough. She took it down and put it in the corner near the fireplace, the only place in the room where Dog was allowed to eat. His snout was in it before she'd completely removed her hand. She patted his head and returned to the table, where she put meat, beans, and pears on a plate.

Unlike Dog, who was wolfing down his food like a starving man, she ate listlessly.

Dog finished his food, and trotted to her side, looking up at her with a begging look in his eyes.

She gave him half of one of her slices of pork, which he swallowed after one quick chew, then, sat back, still begging with his eyes for more.

She laughed, and resumed eating.

When she'd finished her meal, she washed her plate and Dog's bowl, and put the extra beans and pears into two bowls which she covered with plates and put in the cooler. That would be her supper.

A supper she would eat alone, except for Dog's presence. And while she loved the greedy old dog, nothing could take the place of Caleb. From the moment she'd laid eyes on him when he stopped to winter over in her village, she'd known that their spirits were entwined.

She slammed her palm on the table, causing Dog's head to jerk up and his eyes to widen.

"I will not sit here and moan my fate," she said. She looked at Dog. "How would you like to take a trip, Dog?"

"Woof," Dog answered.

## 10.

The weather continued to favor Caleb as far as visibility was concerned. He kept glancing back over his shoulder to keep the bright spot in the mist he knew or assumed to be the sun in the proper place.

For the animals, though, it was a trial. The snow was up to their hocks in most places, acting as a drag on their movement. It was especially hard on the pack animals with their heavy loads, and he found himself stopping frequently to give them time to regain traction and extract themselves from the snow.

He couldn't be sure, but after two hours, he figured he'd gone maybe a mile. At that rate, he feared that he wouldn't make the canyon mouth by nightfall as he desired.

"C'mon, Horse," he said, patting his horse's neck. "It's gon' be tough, but I know you can do it."

Horse snorted, sending plumes of vapor from his nostrils, and strained forward. While he wasn't having as much trouble moving through the snow as the pack horses, it was still a slog. But the big stallion had heart, and if Caleb wanted him to do something, he would do it, or die trying.

Caleb hoped it wouldn't come to that. If the animals became too distressed, whether he made it to the canyon mouth or not, he would stop and make camp, and not just because he cared for his animals. If they faltered or died, he wouldn't be far behind.

He patted Horse's neck once again, and settled in the saddle.

Time seemed to stretch out into infinity. Without a clear view of the sky and the sun, he could only guess at the passage of the minutes. The land around him, coated in an unvarying layer of white, with one snow drift looking exactly like another, he had no way of gauging his speed of travel by the changing landscape around him. The monotonous white surrounding him also had an almost hypnotic effect, and he found himself swaying in the saddle.

His head jerked up and he shook himself.

"Gotta stay awake," he murmured. "Go to sleep out here 'n I'm a goner."

He pinched at his nose and patted his cheeks, but the cold made it feel like he'd been slapped. He shook his head.

"Well, that ain't gon' work."

He tried singing, but while he was the best hunter, trapper, and tracker in Colorado, he couldn't hold a tune in a bucket.

Horse tossed his head and whinnied.

"Okay, I know I can't sing, you old nag," he said. "But I gotta do somethin' to stay awake."

Horse shook his head again.

"Don' wan' me to sing, huh? Guess you gotta point. Sound like a rake against a tin tub."

He could whistle, though, so he started whistling 'Silver Threads Among the Gold,' a simple ditty about a man growing old, but pledging his love. Not too fast, but not too slow, it was just the thing to keep his mind from wandering, and Horse seemed to pick up his pace to keep time with his whistling. After two repetitions of 'Silver Threads,' he launched into "I'll Take You Home Again Kathleen," a similar melody at about the same tempo. Horse whinnied his approval.

Caleb stopped whistling long enough to say, "Well, thank you for your approval, Horse. I always good at whistlin'."

The whistling helped to lift his mood. He no longer felt drowsy. He understood, now, why many of the cow hands he'd met talked about singing to the cattle when they rode night watch on a herd. It wasn't to calm the cows; it was to help them stay awake.

His stomach growled, and he looked behind and up. The bright area of illumination in the gray mist was almost directly overhead.

"Looks like it's gittin' on to midday, Horse. Reckon we oughta stop 'n cook some grub."

He pulled to a stop near a snow-covered grove of trees, so heavily laden with the white stuff he couldn't even tell what kind of trees they were. He decided against making a fire, as much as he would've loved a hot cup of coffee. Time, he felt, was of the essence, so he would eat a cold meal, washing it down with water from his canteen, and press on.

After wrapping the reins of the three horses around the trunk of a small tree that stood apart from the others, he took some jerky and hardtack from his saddle bag, and crouched down to eat. The horses began nosing in the snow in search of grass underneath. Fortunately, the snow wasn't deep, and they were soon rewarded with some limp grass which they hungrily pulled from the frozen ground.

Jerky and hard tack are both hard to eat even when warm. The jerky, if it has been stored a long time, is as tough as boot leather, and hard tack is like trying to bite into a rock. In cold weather they only become harder. Caleb took out his cook pot and poured some water into it from his canteen. He then put a hard tack biscuit in the pot, and squatted there gnawing on the strip of jerky while the biscuit slowly absorbed enough water to make it only leathery rather than rock-hard. He took it out of the water and took alternating bites of bread and meat, with an occasional swig of water until they were gone. They sat in his stomach like a five-pound bag of beans, but there was nothing he could do about it. It took too much time to gather wood, make a fire, cook a meal, clean up, and put the fire out.

He had to get moving.

After stowing his pot away, and scooping snow into his canteen to replace the water he'd used, he pulled the horses away from their meager meal, climbed onto Horse's back, and began plodding onward.

After two more hours of riding, he figured he was within striking distance of the mouth of the canyon. Swirling mist indicated a rise in temperature and air currents told him that narrow mouth that funneled an almost constant breeze into the canyon told him he was probably less than a mile. He smiled. He'd make it before nightfall. Outside the canyon, he'd be on a broad downward-sloping plain and, hopefully, there would be landmarks he could use to set his direction.

He was so happy at the thought of being so close to his goal, he didn't see the dark shapes moving through the mist at first. He didn't see them, in fact, until Horse did a stutter step and whinnied loudly, tossing his head.

"What is it, Horse? You smell somethin/?"

Horse snorted and stopped walking. The pack horses were also snorting and kicking at the snow.

Then, he saw them.

Four dark shapes in a line across his line of travel, about three feet between them. They stood still. He heard a snuffing sound behind him. Looking back over his shoulder, he saw six more shapes, spread out in an irregular line, and moving slowly in his direction.

He didn't need to see them clearly to know what they were.

He was being stalked by a pack of hungry wolves.

*Charles Ray*

## 11.

Flora put on her wool-lined deerskin jacket and went outside to the barn, where she took her horse out of its stall.

"Sorry, old girl," she said. "I hate to make you go outside in such cold, but we must go find Caleb."

The horse whinnied softly, and followed her mistress. Her flanks quivered when the cold air outside the barn hit her.

After tying the horse to one of the corral posts, she went back inside the barn, and pushed the buckboard outside. She then hooked the horse to the buckboard, got up on the seat and drove it to the front of the cabin.

She made several trips back and forth between the cabin and the buckboard., with Dog on her heels for each one, his tail now wagging furiously. In addition to an extra heavy coat and food for a week, she added a keg of water, and Caleb's extra Winchester Model 1873 rifle and two boxes of cartridges. The last thing she did was strap her hunting knife to her waist.

When everything was secure in the buckboard, she looked down at Dog. "Are you ready to go find Caleb, Dog?"

"Woof! Woof!"

"Good. Get up on the seat, and let us go."

The dusting of snow on the ground in front of the cabin made it hard for Dog's feet to get good purchase, so it took him three tries to get up onto the seat. When he finally did, he looked down at Flora with his head cocked to the side as if asking for her praise. She smiled.

"Good work, Dog," she said.

"Woof," he answered.

Laughing, she hoisted herself up onto the seat next to him and grabbed the reins. Flipping them, she got her horse moving forward slowly, heading for the road that ran past the cabin, and then west toward the mountains, which were just visible in the thin mist that hung low over the land.

The road, used a lot by ranchers, farmers, and miners who lived in the flatlands west of their cabin, was muddy and rutted from wagon and horse tracks, forcing her to maintain a slow pace to keep the buckboard from sliding off to the side where the snow was still deep.

A couple of riders approaching her, stopped when they saw that she was a woman alone.

"Howdy, ma'am," said the older rider, a square-jawed man with a flowing white mustache. "Ya Caleb Johnson's wife, ain't ya?"

Since their encounter with three hooligans from Bear Creek who had accosted her, everyone for miles around knew who she was, and treated her with respect.

She nodded at them.

"Yes, I am Flora Johnson," she said.

"Ya mind me askin' why ya out here by yourself, ma'am?"

"My husband went to the mountains to hunt before the snow came. I am afraid he might be hurt, so I am going to look for him."

Worried looks creased the men's faces.

"Ya sure that's a good idea, Miz Johnson," the younger man, a towhead with a wispy growth starting above his upper lip. "It can git kinda dangerous out there."

She patted the rifle propped against the seat and then rubbed Dog's head.

"I think I will be safe," she said. "But I do appreciate your concern."

The two men shared a glance and then tipped their hats to her.

"Well, ma'am," the older one said. "Take care of yourself, 'n when ya find Caleb, tell 'im Jeremiah Cobb 'n Jim Fry said howdy."

"I will do that." She slipped the reins, and the buckboard moved forward.

The two men sat there on their horses watching her.

"I don't know which one of 'em is tougher," the older one said. "Caleb or that Shoshone wife of his."

"I would wanna tangle with either one of 'em," said the younger one. "Ya'd have a better chance agin a grizzly bear."

Chuckling, they turned their horses and resumed their journey to Bear Creek.

*Charles Ray*

## 12.

He had no doubt that the wolf pack was stalking him. Caleb pulled his buffalo rifle from the scabbard and cradled it across his chest. Then, he pulled Horse to a halt, watching how the wolves reacted, both those in front, and the ones coming up behind him.

It would be dangerous to allow them to get in too close. The horses would panic, and he would have his hands full trying to control them while fighting off the pack. He needed to convince them to look for other prey.

The wolves in front stopped when he stopped. He looked back and saw that those behind had also stopped. Probably thinking, insofar as wolves could think, that he was planning to make a run for it.

While they studied them, he studied them. He knew that the four wolves in front were probably the pack leader and the strongest hunters of the pack, probably all males, while the females and younger males were those coming up from behind.

He watched the way the four wolves in front interacted with each other and noticed that, as he would have expected, the largest of the four was being deferred to.

"So, you're the big dog in the pack, eh," he said. "Well, if you waitin' for me to run, you gon' git older and grayer, 'cause Caleb Johnson don' run when he knows it'd jest git 'im killed."

The four wolves prowled back and forth, the three subordinate males walking circles around the pack leader he stood with his ears erect, his eyes on Caleb.

The big wolf raised his muzzle to the sky and let out a long, mournful howl. This galvanized the other three who lined up, one to his left, the other two to his right. They began walking toward Caleb, taking their time. Caleb glanced quickly to his rear and saw that the wolves in the rear had also begun to advance.

It was time to act.

He had only one chance. If it worked, he was home free, if it failed, he was going to be in the battle of his life . . . for his life.

He raised his rifle and centered the front sight on the spot where the big wolf's left foreleg joined his body. Estimating the range at just under a hundred yards, he raised the sight slightly to compensate for the drop of the slug over that distance. He took a slow, deep breath and began letting it out slowly. Near the end of his exhale he squeezed the trigger.

The bang of the buffalo rifle was loud in his ears, and the butt of the rifle slammed against his shoulder like a mule kick, but he held it steady and swung right, aiming at the second animal in the line, and fired as soon as the bulk of the wolf's body was in his sight.

All of this took less than three seconds.

The 'bang-bang' of the rifle was followed almost immediately by the two wolves dropping to the snow, bright red blood spurting from the wounds in their chests. The remaining two wolves stopped and looked around, confused and unsettled by the sudden noise, and by the sight of their leader lying still in the snow with a growing red shape forming beneath his body.

Caleb didn't waste time checking on his kills. He knew his slugs had found their targets. He whirled around in the saddle, his thighs tight to keep Horse's shying from throwing him off, and raised the rifle again.

"Easy, old boy," he said. "I'm keepin' them wolves from makin' a lunch outta you."

Horse snorted and stopped jumping. The pack horses, eyes wide with terror, pawed at the snow.

The wolves behind him had slowed their forward movement when he shot, but were now bounding toward him, unaware that they were now a leaderless pack They were still over a hundred yards back, but at the speed they were running, it would only be seconds before they reached him.

He let them lope a few more steps, and aimed at the wolf in the lead. Smoke from the end of the barrel blocked his view for a second, but when it cleared, he saw the animal down, and the others scattering to right and left to get away from this strange sound that seemed to be coming from their prey.

Just to make sure, Caleb shot one of the fleeing animals, catching it in the flank. The force of the slug caused it to veer to the side, crashing into one of its companions. The bumped wolf growled and snapped at his attacker, but that animal was already dead, or very close to death, and lay on its side. When Caleb turned back to the wolves in front, he saw that the two surviving wolves were already heading away from him.

He made a full circle, watching as both groups faded into the distance. He smiled.

"That'll teach you to mess with Caleb Johnson," he yelled.

He gave them a few minutes to make sure they hadn't circled back, then nudged Horse's flanks.

All three horses balked when they approached the two dead wolves, the combination of wolf and blood smell triggering a desire to flee, but Caleb patted Horse's neck and kept a tight hold on the reins of the pack horses.

"Settle down, all of y'all," he said. "Them wolves ain't gon' bother you none. It oughta be a smooth ride from here to home."

Horse tossed his head and neighed. Without Caleb's urging, he quickened his step.

## 13.

The sun was low in the sky when the canyon mouth came into sight. Caleb breathed a sigh of relief. It might be dark by the time he found a suitable place to camp, but out there on the open, with the bulk of the mountains at his back, he would be able to make his way home with his eyes closed.

He patted Horse's neck.

"We made it, old friend," he said. "Shouldn't be more'n three days home from here." He looked around, especially toward the east. While snow covered everything, it didn't seem quite as deep as it had been in the box canyon. "Looks like we gon' be able to move a bit faster, too."

Horse responded with a prancing step that caused the pack horses' reins to tighten in Caleb's grip.

"Hey, hold up there, Horse. Don' forgit, we got two horses with us that's totin' a mite more weight than you. So, step lively, but not quite so fast, okay?"

Horse neighed and tossed his head, but slowed his pace.

"That's better," Caleb said, patting his neck again. "But I know how you feel. I'd like nothin' better'n to be home right now."

Horse settled into a steady pace, not a canter, but faster than a simple walk. The pack horses resisted at first, but finally settled into the same tempo. Caleb sat easy in the saddle, letting his horse lead the way. Horse was clearly the boss of the situation, and he felt confident that his trusty old companion knew what he was doing.

Time went by all too slowly in his mind, but the wind had stopped blowing and the snow was no longer falling, and he could now figure out where he was by landmarks that he could see through the light haze that hung over everything. He welcomed the mist, because that was an indication that the temperature was rising, and that would mean the snow would begin melting, making travel a lot easier.

It was getting dark, though, and he needed to find a place to camp for the night.

He came to an ideal spot just as it began to get dark. A broad area with a few snow-covered trees. A nearby stream was covered by a layer of ice. He stopped near a small stand of young black oak trees, dismounted, and tied the horses to low-hanging limbs.

The few dead and broken pieces of wood he found were soggy, but by digging into the hard earth with his knife, he was able to find a few pieces that miraculously had dry centers. Even some of the soggy pieces he'd found beneath the snow were relatively dry in the center, so after stacking a pile near a circle he'd cleared in the snow, he began carving several sticks to expose the drier core. When he had enough to get a fire going, he stacked and lit them. It took a while, and the damp wood put out more smoke than he liked, but he finally had a nice little blaze going. He then shaved the surface of several more pieces of wood and added them.

From some smaller sticks, he constructed a tripod from which he hung his pot for cooking beans, and his coffee pot into which he'd put snow, coffee and chicory. He then took out his skillet and tossed in four strips of pork. He held the skillet over the fire until the meat was brown, and he had an eighth of an inch of grease. He put the meat on his plate and put two hardtack biscuits in the grease and held it over the fire to moisten and heat the bread. That done, he put the biscuits on the plate next to the pork and put it aside.

While the coffee brewed, he walked to the pack horses and removed the bag of oats he'd brought along and poured three small piles in the snow in front of each horse. They whinnied their thanks and began eating. He put the bag back and went back to find that his coffee was ready.

He poured a cup and blew on it before taking a sip. It still burned his lips, but he ignored the burn and took a second sip.

Then he picked up his plate and began eating.

With nothing to do but go to sleep, he took his time with his food. Then, he used snow to clean the plate, skillet and pot, and poured himself another cup of coffee.

He hadn't bothered building a lean-to, instead, he pushed snow up to make a three-sided structure, with the open side down wind of the prevailing winds. He then put a deerskin down and a blanket over that, with another blanket to sleep under. It wasn't as comfortable or as warm of his bed at home, but it would do. He finished his coffee, rinsed out the cup, banked the fire, and wrapped the blanket around himself.

Lying back, with his saddle as a pillow, he gazed up at stars he could just barely see through the mist, his thoughts wandering across the snow-covered plain to a cabin, and the woman who waited for him there.

As he drifted off to sleep, Flora's face was the last image in his mind.

*Charles Ray*

## 14.

Flora made good time the first two days of her journey, unhitching her horse at night and tying her to the rear wheel of the buckboard, and then crawling in and snuggling in the bags of supplies with Dog nestled against her back and the rifle at her side. She'd built a fire each time to cook her supper, but put it out as soon as she finished eating.

She knew roughly where Caleb had gone to hunt meat for the winter. He had described the box canyon in which herds of deer grazed, and the general route to get to it. Once at the canyon, unless she met him on the way, she hoped that dog would be able to locate him. She'd brought along one of his old shirts to provide the animal with a scent to trace.

Her plan seemed simple, but she knew that even a simple plan could go haywire easily. She didn't let that get her down, though. Things would work the way she'd planned, or they wouldn't. If things went wrong, she would change her plan and try something else. She *would* find Caleb, though. That was the only thing on her mind as she fell asleep each night.

It was on the third day, with a horse that was tired from the unaccustomed weight of the buckboard over roads that hadn't been heavily traveled and were either under a half-inch of snow, or dotted with puddles of icy mud where the rising temperatures had melted the snow in the wagon ruts.

Even Dog was starting to fret. Occasionally making a whining noise as the wagon hit yet another rut, jostling them on the unpadded seat.

"It will not be long, Dog," she said after he'd moaned for the third time in an hour. "We will soon be on a part of the road that does not get many wagons. It will be smoother, I promise."

Dog yawned and leaned against her arm.

It was getting late in the day, and they'd only stopped once to eat a cold meal, and allow Dog to run around in the snow to stretch his legs.

"We will stop for the night soon," she said. "I have a feeling that tomorrow will be a better day. Tonight, I will cook something special for you. Would you like that?"

"Woof!"

Dog's tail thumped loudly against the buckboard seat.

Caleb had often told her that Dog understood everything they said to him. She hadn't sure, other than when she mentioned food if that was true. But since the trip started, and she had said at the beginning that she wanted him to stay on the buckboard with her, he hadn't once jumped off to chase small animals. Even when a large jackrabbit darted across the road in front of them, Dog barked, but remained still beside her.

"Maybe Caleb is right. Maybe you do understand everything we say."

"Woof!"

She patted his head, getting her gloved hand licked in response to the gesture.

As a gust of wind blew across the road, kicking up a light dusting of snow, she decided that it was time to stop for the day.

Finding a place where she felt it would be safe to leave the road was always a challenge. In places, there were ditches alongside the road, now filled with snow, and should she get the wheels of the buckboard stuck in one, she might not be able to get it out.

She'd worked out a way to avoid such a mishap. When she saw a nice flat area that would be a good place to stop for the night, she stopped the buckboard.

"Okay, Dog," she said. "Ready to help me see if it's safe to get off the road here?"

"Woof!"

Dog jumped from his seat on the buckboard, landing in a snowdrift and sinking in up to his belly. He scrambled out and stood gingerly on top of the pile of snow.

Flora laughed and stepped down herself, careful where she put her feet. Instead of her usual moccasins, she wore a pair of mid-thigh-high leather boots that Caleb had insisted she buy during one of their trips to Bear Creek, telling her that some of the terrain around their cabin was too rough for her moccasins, especially in the winter when ice and slush was everywhere. She'd objected, but went along with him, and now was glad she had. She sank in to her ankles. If she'd been wearing her moccasins, they would've become filled with snow, and she'd be in danger of frostbite, which would be deadly this far from home.

She then walked to the area she thought would be a good point to leave the road and stepped carefully onto the snow. Her feet were still ankle-deep in the snow. She kept walking until she was standing in snow less than half an inch deep. She nodded, turned, and went back to the buckboard.

Dog, meanwhile, was walking around in wide circles, stopping occasionally to urinate to mark their new territory, which made her laugh while

at the same time she was happy that he marked
such an ambitious tract so that she wouldn't have
to smell the ammonia-odor of his urine all night.

When he'd finished, he came back and
followed her as she walked back to the buckboard
and carefully guided the horse by the reins onto
her chosen camp ground. She stopped it in the
center of a roughly oval area, near a small
evergreen tree to which she tied the horse after
she'd unhitched her from the buckboard.

She then walked to a stand of larger trees just
outside the oval where she was able to find
enough fallen branches to make a decent fire.

The ones that were too big, she broke in half,
and saved several long, slender ones to construct
a tripod to hang her pot on. In minutes she had a
good fire going and a pot of coffee brewing. She
then began rummaging in the burlap bag of food
in the buckboard, looking for something to keep
her promise to Dog that she would prepare
something special.

She'd brought a small chunk of beef and a slab
of pork, and several cans of beans and pears, as
well as a large loaf of cornmeal bread that she'd
baked. She decided on pork, which was easier to
cook, and for some reason was Dog's favorite
meat other than smoked venison. She cut off
three thick slices from the slab and put them in
the skillet, and balanced it on two flat rocks she'd
found at the edge of the fire. Using the same knife,
she opened a can of beans and dumped them into
the pot, and hung it over the fire. She put the
pears aside, to be opened when she'd finished
eating her main meal, knowing that if she opened
them and Dog caught the sweet scent, he would
worry her for some, which Caleb had strictly
forbidden her to do.

As the coffee boiled and the food cooked slowly, she folded up a deerskin and sat cross-legged on it, staring into the flames and wondering what Caleb was having for his supper.

When the coffee smelled ready, she took the pot off the fire and filled her cup. After putting the pot back over the fire, she picked up the cup and held it under her nose, letting the woody aroma of the coffee and the sweet smell of chicory tickle the insides of her nostrils. Before marrying Caleb, she had never drunk coffee, and had recoiled at the first sip he'd given her. But in time, she had come to love a warm cup of coffee to start the day, and another to end it, as much as he did. She blew on it to cool it down, and took a sip, letting it linger on her tongue for a few moments before swallowing.

The pork, sizzling in the skillet, had started curling up at the ends, and the bottom portion that she could see was light brown. Caleb had cautioned her to always cook pork thoroughly to make sure any worms that might be in it were killed. Not that the thought of worms bothered her. In times of scarcity of game, her village had on occasion eating the thick white grubs they found beneath rotting logs, or roasted locusts over the fire. It was an acquired taste. But Caleb had said that the worms sometimes found in pork would make a person sick, and sometimes even kill them, so she was always careful when she cooked pork. Why the same thing was not true of beef, he could not explain, but he would often cook a thick piece of beef until it was brown on the outside, but still pink, and sometimes red, in the center. She had to admit, though, that it tasted really good cooked that way.

But Dog liked pork, so pork it would be. Cooked nice and brown, with the edges just getting crispy. She used a spoon to dip out some of the pork grease and stirred it into the beans. Then, she went to the buckboard and took out a small bag of sugar. She poured a small mound of the white crystals into the palm of her hand and dropped it into the beans, stirring until grease and sugar were fully absorbed by the plump red beans. She then put two squares of the corn loaf into the skillet, letting it soak up the grease. She took them out, and first put a piece of pork, three spoons of beans and one of the corn squares into a bowl for Dog. His ears perked up when he saw her putting food into *his* dish, but a stern look from her kept him rooted to a spot three feet from the fire. She put the dish down on the side away from him to let it cool, and filled her own plate.

She picked up his bowl and blew on it until she felt it was warm, but not so warm as to burn his mouth, and then put it down near him, and nodded.

Dog dived at the bowl like it was a rabbit frozen in fear, and began eating as only a hungry dog can eat, gobbling up large quantities of meat, bread, and beans together, chewing twice, and swallowing.

By the time she'd filled her own plate, he was licking the bottom of the bowl clean.

"You are worse than Caleb, Dog," she said. "I spend so much time preparing you a fine meal, and you swallow it down in a few bites. Are you not grateful?"

"Woof!"

"Very well. I accept your thanks. Now, sit quietly while I eat my food."

He sat on his haunches, looking at her with his begging-for-food look, his head dipping up and down, following the motion of her hand as she moved her food from her plate to her mouth.

She ate all but a small bit of pork, a few beans, and some crumbs, which she spooned into his bowl.

"Woof," he said, and polished it off in two big bites.

"Now, I will clean up and bank the fire, and we will get some rest. Get into the buckboard."

Dog ran to the rear of the buckboard and jumped up, grabbing the back rail with his forepaws and then levering himself up and over. He lay down, waiting for her to join him.

When everything was cleaned and put away, and the fire was banked—for some reason, she felt the need of the fire this night—she took the rifle from the front of the buckboard and climbed into the back.

She pulled the deerskin blanket over them and settled down to sleep, partially comforted by the warmth of Dog at her back, but still thinking of Caleb.

"Caleb, my husband," she whispered before she drifted off to sleep. "What are you doing tonight?"

# Charles Ray

## 15.

Caleb tossed and turned all night. Finally, must before daybreak, he gave up trying to sleep. He threw off his blanket and got the fire, which had almost died, going, and started a pot of coffee.

While the coffee was brewing, he tossed some pork and a can of beans into the pot and put it on the fire, not wanting to have to spend too much time cleaning his gear. He had miles to go, and wanted to get an early start.

He gave the horses some more oats, noticing as he did that, he had just about enough for one more day, two if he put them on short rations, which he was reluctant to do given the loads the pack horses were carrying.

"Well, if I'm lucky, down past the foothills they didn't git as much snow, 'n you fellas can find some fall grass to graze on. Figure we oughta be makin' it gittin' on to night fall.

The horses snorted and began eating the meager piles of grain. Horse stopped eating long enough to look at him with an accusing glint in his eyes.

"Don' be lookin' at me like that, Horse," Caleb said. "Ain't my fault the weather took a bad turn."

Horse snorted and resumed eating.

Caleb went back to the fire and quickly wolfed down his own food.

After cleaning up and stowing gear, he loaded the pack horses and saddled Horse.

"Okay, here's how it's gon' be," he said. "I wanna git outta the foothills well 'fore dark, so we gon' be pushin' hard today. Y'all up to it."

None of the horses made a sound except for Horse's hooves stamping the snow.

"Well, I ain't heard nobody say no, so let's git ridin'"

He started off at a fast walk, and when the horses didn't try to lag, pushed Horse into a canter, a gait that he could keep up just about all day if necessary. He wasn't so sure the pack horses could, though, so he planned on stopping every hour for a few minutes to let them catch their wind.

The mist seemed to be clearing. In places he could see patches of slate-blue sky, and there was no wind beyond a gentle breeze blowing against the back of his neck. In the distance, he could see a herd of elk, led by a buck with a magnificent rack. Any other time, he would've made a side trip and taken one of the younger bucks for meat, but not today. He wanted to get home.

After half an hour of riding, he found himself whistling a tune whose name he couldn't remember, but the melody just popped into his head. Horse seemed to like it. He did a little prancing step now and then and tossed his head like the horses on parade before the traveling rodeo that came to Bear Creek every other year or so.

He was finally feeling good.

"I'm gon' be seein' my Flora soon, Horse," he said, patting the big stallion's neck. "Whatcha think 'bout that?"

Horse snorted.

## 16.

Flora was getting drowsy. She'd awakened before sunrise, had a quick breakfast, and got an early start. Dog, asleep at her back, whined, stretched, and yawned when she woke him, and seemed reluctant to leave the warmth of the blanket they shared, but she finally roused him with a promise of food, the only thing other than a small animal sunning past that would pull him out of a sleeping position.

Dog jumped from the back of the buckboard, and began following her as she stoked up the fire and got food from her bag.

He sat near her, his tail swishing over the snow, as she began cooking strips of pork in a skillet while beans bubbled in a pot hanging nearby. She put two hard tack biscuits in the skillet with the pork. At that point, his tongue came out and wagged as fast as his tail.

"Be patient, Dog," she said. "You cannot eat the food until I finish cooking it."

"Woof," he responded, which she knew meant, 'No, I can eat it raw."

"But, I cannot, or I choose not to, so you must wait."

He whined at her. She smiled.

When the beans were hot, the pork was brown, and the hard tack no longer so hard, she put one piece of meat, one biscuit, and two spoons of beans in his bowl, which, as usual, she put down so that she crouched between it and him, to let it cool while she filled her own plate.

That done, she picked his bowl up and blew on it until satisfied it wouldn't burn his mouth, and put it down in front of him. He looked at her with his head cocked to the side.

"Woof!"

"Yes, you may eat," she said.

He did, with his usual aggressive, loud, and sloppy behavior. She ate quickly, too, but with les noise and mess, but he still finished before she was half done and began looking longingly at her plate.

"Not this morning, Dog. I am hungry, and will need my strength today. We should be meeting Caleb soon, but only if we ride long and hard."

He looked disappointed.

When she had finished her food and coffee, and washed and stowed the containers and utensils, she ordered him back to his seat beside her on the buckboard and set out, still heading west and following a road that was less rutted, but also, because it was less traveled, was less smooth overall. The ride was bumpy.

In her effort to find a smoother part of the road, and in her fatigued state, she wasn't as careful making sure she stayed away from the edge of the road.

It was when she felt the buckboard tip precariously to the right, causing Dog to scramble to stay on the seat, she did not at first understand what was happening. The buckboard stopped shaking. Her horse strained in the traces but was unable to move it, and then when her brain finally processed it all, she was crestfallen.

She was stuck in the snow-filled ditch that ran alongside the road.

Carefully, she climbed over the left side of the buckboard and dropped to the ground. She walked around the back to look. What she saw felt like a mule kick to her stomach. Both wheels on the right side were stuck up to the axle. From the dark stains she saw in the snow, she knew that underneath it was sludge and mud, the kind that sucks a horse's hooves or a wagon wheel down and clings to them like glue.

She walked back to the front and tried calming her frightened horse.

"Calm down, old girl," she said. "I will pull your rein. See if you can pull the buckboard from the mud."

She pulled slowly, and the horse strained until the muscles of her shoulders and haunches bunched up, but the buckboard didn't budge. She went to the back and put her shoulders against it.

"Go, girl, pull!"

But the buckboard was held fast in the mud. Other than a slot rocking motion when she pushed and the horse pulled, it did not move.

She ground her teeth and tried again, and again, and again.

She was determined to get the buckboard back on the road.

The mud was just as determined in its brainless way that she would not.

# Charles Ray

## 17.

The wind had stopped, the sky was clearing, and the snow was melting, especially on the road. It was messy, but Caleb was happy. He could now make good time. With luck, he would be home in two more days, three tops.

He hummed to himself, in tune with the up and down movement as Horse clopped along in a steady canter, glancing over his shoulder every few minutes to make sure the pack horses weren't being overtaxed. They too, though, seemed to sense the nearness of home, and both kept pace with Horse.

A strange thing happens when you're riding a well-trained horse under good weather conditions and a lack of threats to your welfare. You tend to drop into a state of semi-sleep, a place between being awake and being sound asleep, when you're unconsciously aware of the real world outside your dreams, and your dreams, but unable to distinguish between the two.

That is where Caleb found himself. Gently swaying with the up and down movements of Horse's canter, soothed by a gentle breeze that kissed the back of his neck, and almost hypnotized by the rhythmic sound of the horse's hooves as they penetrated the thinning layer of snow and struck the ground beneath, making dull thudding sounds, he was almost unaware of the passage of time.

In the back of his mind he was aware, though, that allowing himself to be lulled into a state of somnolence was dangerous. In this near-sleep state, there was a chance of riding into a hazardous situation, and not being able to react quickly enough to avoid serious injury. He knew that Horse picked up on his moods, and if he was drowsy and inattentive, Horse might do the same, causing him not to watch where he put his hooves. Even at the relatively slow speed of his canter, should a hoof land in a hole, or on a loose rock, it could break his leg, leaving Caleb no alternative but to put his old companion out of his misery, and then having to decide what to throw away because he would have to ride one of the pack horses.

This realization hit the forefront of his brain like a rock, causing him to shudder and shake his head vigorously.

"Whoa, gotta stay alert," he murmured, but Horse had heard 'whoa,' and he came to a sudden stop, rocking Caleb forward, waking him even more. "No, Horse, I didn't mean for you to stop. Giddyap. We got to get home."

Horse slowly began moving forward. Caleb began whistling. Horse resumed the steady canter. Behind them, the pack horses snorted their displeasure at the interruption of their own movement.

To keep from becoming drowsy again, Caleb whistled, hummed, and talked to himself, all the while scanning the snow-covered terrain around him, paying particular attention to that in front of him. The last thing he needed now was an accident. He hoped that his heightened awareness was communicating itself to Horse.

It seemed to be.

Horse had settled into an easy gait, one that wouldn't tire him but that would steal eat up the miles. Caleb knew the animals, especially Horse, were anxious to get home as he was.

Satisfied that he was back in a suitable mental state, he began to examine his surroundings, not looking for danger, for he didn't expect any problems out on the open plain, but to catalog landmarks for future trips to the area. But he looked also just to enjoy the view. Here, coming out of the foothills and onto the plain, broken only by a few hills here and there, such as the one on which his cabin was built, was some of the most beautiful scenery in the world—in his opinion.

Oregon had been nice, but the mountains there lacked the majestic stature of Colorado's peaks.

Colorado also had, in his opinion, a greater variety of wildlife, ranging from the mule deer to magnificent elks to mountain lions. The skies had hawks, ravens, and eagles at the top of the avian food chain, and hundreds of smaller birds that at times created an amazing palate of colors against Colorado's brilliant blue sky.

At the moment he thought about the great numbers of animals, birds, and plants his home had, he saw a jackrabbit, a big one, bounding across the snow. Then, he saw a shadow closing in on the rabbit. When he looked up, he saw a merlin, a small hawk that came south from Canada in the winter, closing in on the rabbit that was almost half its size. He watched with interest as the rabbit ran a zig-zag course in its effort to escape the merlin's talons. But the bird, with quick flaps of its wings, matched the rabbit's course until the inevitable final encounter, when its talons sank into the flesh at the back of the poor rabbit's neck. Because of its size, weight, and struggling, the hawk couldn't lift it. Not that it had to. With several quick jabs from its sharp beak, it severed an artery and began pulling at the rabbit's flesh before its twitching even stopped.

Many people would've been repulsed by the scene, but Caleb realized that this was the order of things, and viewed it dispassionately. In the wild, some animals fed on other animals, and, as had been the case in his encounters with the mountain lion and the wolves, it sometimes came down to kill or be killed.

He shrugged and kept riding.

At midday, he stopped long enough to feed each horse a handful of what was left of the grain, and get a piece of jerky from his pack, which he ate while he rode, taking the occasional sip of water from his canteen. He knew he would be ravenous at supper, but he wanted to put as many miles behind him as possible before stopping for the night.

Somewhere around the middle of the afternoon, based on the position of the sun, he saw something dark against the snow about a half a mile ahead. He stopped and squinted.

From the distance, he couldn't make out details, but it appeared to be a small wagon or cart nearly tipped over. He could see one horse, and a small figure pushing at the cart.

"Looks like somebody done run off the road, Horse," he said. "Well, it's on our way, so I reckon we oughta go see if we can give 'em a hand.

## 18.

Flora had all but exhausted her strength and had been unable to move the buckboard an inch. Her back and arms hurt, and she was breathing hard. Her horse also seemed to be fatigued and on the point of panic from being tethered to this devilish device that refused to move and was at an angle that caused the shafts to rub painfully against her flanks.

Anyone else would've long since given up. But it was not in Flora's nature to accept defeat. She believed that the Great Spirit would look out for those who lived in the right way, and that there was always a way. She just had to find it.

Or, it would find her.

Just before leaning in against the buckboard again in her effort to get it out of the ditch, she just happened to look up. She saw a group of riders way off in the distance, and they appeared to be coming her way.

She looked up at the sky, and smiled.

"Thank you, Oh Great Spirit," she said. "You have sent help to a daughter in need."

She leaned against the buckboard and wept quietly.

*Charles Ray*

## 19.

As Caleb got closer to the wagon, he saw that it was a buckboard with one horse, and that it had indeed run into the ditch and gotten stuck. Too deeply mired in the mud and slush for the single horse to pull it free. He could see the slight figure, swathed in a long coat, standing at the rear of the buckboard.

"Now, there's one fella that ain't too smart," he said. "Comin' out here in weather like this by himself. We hadn't come 'long, poor fella mighta froze to death way out here."

While it would delay his getting home, there was no question that Caleb would stop and help the stranded traveler. The only people who wouldn't were outlaws on the run, and even they might when a posse wasn't hot on their tails.

That was the way of the west. Helping a stranger in distress was the money you paid into the bank of goodwill, earning interest when you were in trouble and a stranger gave you a helping hand.

"C'mon, Horse, let's go help this fella git his wagon outta that ditch."

He pressed his knees against Horse's side. The animal's canter changed to a slow gallop. Caleb knew this would put strain on the pack horses, but he had no idea how long this poor unfortunate person had been out in the cold. It was important to get him on his way as soon as possible. The pack horses would get a rest while he and Horse helped get the wagon back on the road.

When he was less than a quarter mile away, he saw a large dark shape bounding toward him through the snow. At first, it looked like a wolf, which puzzled him. Why, he thought, would a wolf be hunting alone, and why would it be coming toward him instead of the stranded stranger. He pulled his buffalo rifle from its sheath and held it across the pommel of his saddle.

Horse never broke stride, which he found strange. Horse hated wolves even more than he did.

Then, as the running shape drew nearer, his mouth gaped open in astonishment.

He recognized Dog, coming toward him, barking loudly and sending sprays of snow off in all directions. Then, his expression turned to one of alarm as he realized that the small *man* that he thought he'd been looking at could only be one person. Flora! *What in blazes is that woman of mine doin' way out here?*

When Dog reached him, he pulled back on Horse's reins, stopping him. Dog barked and began running in circles around Caleb and the three horses. Horse tossed his head back and whinnied a greeting. Caleb dismounted and knelt in the snow. Dog ran up to him, put his forepaws on Caleb's shoulder and began licking his face.

"Dog, what the hell you 'n Flora doin' out here by yourselves?"

"Woof, woof!"

Dog dropped to all fours and turned in Flora's direction. He looked back over his shoulder at Caleb.

"Woof!"

"Yeah, I know," Caleb said. "She done got the buckboard stuck in a ditch 'n need help to git out. You g'on back 'n let 'er know I'm comin'."

"Woof," Dog said, and bounded off, back in Flora's direction.

Caleb remounted.

"C'mon, Horse, Flora's in trouble."

Horse broke into a gallop before Caleb could even knee his sides.

When Caleb arrived at the buckboard, Flora was standing near her horse, trying to calm it while, at the same time, looking toward Caleb.

"Hello, husband," she said. "Could you please help me get this buckboard back on the road?"

Caleb dismounted and ran to her. He put his arms around her waist and pulled her against his body. She snaked one hand around his waist, while still stroking the horse with the other.

His heart beat loudly, and he had difficulty breathing. It took him several minutes to regain his composure. When he did, he released her from his embrace and stepped back a pace.

"Flora, what in blue blazes you doin' out here?"

She looked up at him with a steely gaze.

"You were late coming home, and the snowfall at the cabin was heavy, so I thought it might be even heavier in the mountains," she said. "I was worried about you."

"So, you come out here with one horse 'n Dog as your only protection?"

She walked to the front of the buckboard and removed the rifle.

"No, I had this." She patted the knife strapped to her waist. "And, this."

Caleb laughed.

"Well, I reckon you was armed for bear all right. Still, it wudn't smart to come out here by yourself. If I hadna come along, you coulda froze to death."

"Hmph. Do you think that a Shoshone woman cannot take care of herself? I have lived through worse. We once had a snowfall like this in our village, but we women still had to go out to gather wood for the fires."

"Yeah, reckon I forgits sometime that you ain't no soft crinoline-wearin' lady like some of them women in Bear Creek."

"What about you, husband? Did you have trouble when the snow came? You were in the mountains alone. You could also have frozen."

"Like you, I seen worse. I spent most of my life in these mountains. I know how to survive. My only worry was you back at the cabin all alone."

She nodded.

"So, we both worried. But the Great Spirit has looked over us. Now, we can go home. But I sense that you are not telling me everything that happened to you in the mountains."

He laughed again.

"Dang. Can't keep nothin' from you, can I? I'll tell you all about it, but first, we gotta git this buckboard back on the road. I'll unhitch your horse, 'n take the loads off my pack horses. The two of 'em oughta be able to pull this thing out easy. Then, we load my stuff on the buckboard, tie your horse 'n mine to the back 'n go home."

"That would be a good idea," she said.

With the two pack horses replacing Flora's horse in the traces, and with Caleb pushing from behind, the buckboard was back on the road and pointed toward home in ten minutes. It took another half hour to put his gear, including the two mule deer carcasses in with Flora's supplies and then tie her horse and Horse to the back of the buckboard.

Caleb started to get in on the driver's side, but Flora laid a hand on his arm.

"Do you mind if I drive, husband?" she asked.

He bowed and took her hand to help her up.

"Not at all, wife," he said.

When she was settled, he walked around to the other side, only to find Dog sitting on the seat next to her, leaving him precious little room.

She smiled down at him.

"He has come to like riding up here," she said. "I do not think he likes the snow very much."

"Any way I can git 'im to ride on the outside so I can set next to you?"

"Woof!"

"I think he is saying no," she said.

*Charles Ray*

## 20.

Unlike many of the men he knew, Caleb had no problem with being a passenger with a woman driving, especially a woman with Flora's skills. He did, though, have issues with sharing his seat, and proximity to his wife, with Dog.

Each time he tried nudging Dog into the back of the buckboard, he was rewarded with a whine at first, and when that didn't stop his nudging, Dog would growl and snap at his elbow.

"Dagnabit, Dog," he said. "You'd be a whole lot more comfortable in the back with all that soft stuff to lie on."

"And, two deer carcasses to chew on," Flora said, glancing at him with a devilish smile on her face.

Caleb rapped his knuckles against his forehead.

"Shoot. I plumb forgot about that meat." He snapped his fingers. "Maybe we can stop, 'n I can wrap 'em up real tight so he can't get at 'em. Then, I can talk 'im into layin' down back there."

Flora shook her head.

"If you must," she said. "But if he gets a smell of the meat, I don't think you have anything thick enough or strong enough to keep him out."

She pulled the buckboard to a stop, and sat with her hands in her lap.

"I take you sittin' there to mean I gotta do this myself," Caleb said.

She smiled.

"If I do not keep my hands on the reins, how do we make sure the horses do not get spooked and start running?"

Caleb knew that was highly unlikely, but not impossible, so he just shrugged.

"Okay, I'll get it done as fast as I can."

He nudged Dog and crawled over the back of the seat.

The two deer carcasses were partially uncovered, and the wind blowing in their faces was probably the only reason Dog hadn't already smelled them. He shifted things around, putting the carcasses at the very bottom of the piles of his gear, and then put Flora's bags on top of that, leaving a depression in the middle of one of the bags just big enough for Dog to lie comfortably. Then, he was hit with an inspiration. He knew that the one thing Dog could never resist, other than chasing rabbits and squirrels, was food. He rummaged around in his bag until he found the remnant of a slab of dried beef. Using his knife, he cut it into three pieces and put them in the depression.

"Hey, Dog," he said, looking back over his shoulder. "Look what I found."

He moved aside and pointed to the three hunks of meat.

Dog's head cocked to the side and he looked at Caleb instead of where he was pointing.

Caleb picked up one of the pieces of meat and waved it toward the now-alerted animal, who had picked up the scent. In a flash, Dog bounded over the back of the seat and skillfully snatched the meat from Caleb's hand. While he busily gnawed away at the tough meat, covering the other two with his forepaws, Caleb scrambled over the back of the seat and sat next to Flora, not leaving enough space between them to insert a piece of foolscap.

Flora laughed.

"Caleb Johnson, you are an evil man to trick that poor animal like that."

Caleb shrugged.

"It ain't like he ain't gittin' somethin' outta the trade," he said. "He'll be happily gnawin' on that meat for 'least an hour, 'n after he finishes eatin', he's likely to drop off to sleep."

She patted his thigh.

"It is still an evil thing to do." She smiled. "But I would rather have you sitting next to me than Dog. You're not as warm as he is, but there is more of what warmth you do have."

He put his arms around her shoulders.

"I can do this, too," he said.

"Yes. Dog cannot do that." She tilted her head against his shoulder. "This is much better. Now, tell me about your hunting trip."

"You sure you want to hear 'bout that. Ain't all that much happened."

"I do not believe you. I see a glint in your eye that is always there when you are keeping things from me. I believe you had a great adventure."

"Well, I reckon it was kinda interestin' at that."

"I knew it. Now, tell me."

Caleb cleared his throat and hugged her tighter.

"Well, it all started with this hungry old mountain lion."

*Charles Ray*

# AUTHOR'S NOTE

Those who have read some of my other works will note that the Books by this Author pages that follow are missing quite a few, most notably the Adventures of Deputy US Marshal Bass Reeves, and Texas Ranger J.D. Pettit. Unfortunately, my old publisher, which was the label that issued those titles, went out of business, and all of my books with them disappeared into that oblivion reserved for books out of print.

I'm keeping my fingers crossed, though, that arrangements can be made to republish them at some point in the near future. In the meantime, my books by this label will continue to be available—hopefully—far into the future.

I'm especially proud of this current Caleb Johnson Mountain Man story. Thanks to Nick Wale, the world's greatest publicist, I based Caleb on a historical fiction book I wrote several years ago, and so far, readers seem to like the character, which is nice, because I really like getting inside Caleb's head for his adventures.

*Charles Ray*

# BOOKS BY THIS AUTHOR

**Al Pennyback mysteries**

*Color Me Dead*
*Memorial to the Dead*
*Deadline*
*Dead, White, and Blue*
*A Good Day to Day*
*The Day the Music Died*
*Die, Sinner*
*Deadly Emotions*
*Death by Design*
*Till Death Do Us part*
*Deadly Dose*
*Dead Man's Cove*
*Dead Men Don't Answer*
*Deadly Paradise*
*Kiss of Death*
*Death in White Satin*
*Death and Taxis*
*Deadbeat*
*A Deadly Wind Blows*
*Death Wish*
*Deadly Vendetta*
*A Time to Kill, A Time to Die*
*Dead Ringer*
*Death of Innocence*
*Dead Reckoning*
*Murder on the Menu*
*Over My Dead Body*
*Bad Girls Don't Die*
*A Deal to Die For*
*The Dead Blonde in the Red Bikini*
*Return to Dead Man's Cove*

**Ed Lazenby mysteries**

*Butterfly Effect*
*Coriolis Effect*
*The Cat in the Hatbox*
*Negative Side Effects*

*Murder is as Easy as ABC*
*Body of Evidence*
*Who Killed Henry Hawkins?*
*Skeleton in the Closet*

## Buffalo Soldier

*Trial by Fire*
*Homecoming*
*Incident at Cactus Junction*
*Peacekeepers*
*Renegade*
*Escort Duty*
*Battle at Dead Man's Gulch*
*Yosemite*
*Comanchero*
*Range War*
*Mob Justice*
*Chasing Ghosts*
*The Piano*
*Family Feud*
*The Lost Expedition*
*The Iron Horse*
*Park Patrol*

## Jacob Blade: Vigilante

*Avenging Angel*
*Vengeance is Mine*
*Hot Lead, Cold Steel*
*The Vigilante From Texas*
*Hell in the High Country*
*Last State to Mesa Grande*
*Shootout at Heartbreak Ridge*
*A Fine Day for Dying*
*Vigilante League*
*Last Man Standing*
*Bullet from the Vigilante*
*The Guns of Jacob Blade*
*Vigilante Killer on the Run*
*Cold Steel*
*Heartbreak Ridge Shootout*
*The Last Stage Heading to Mesa Grande*
*The Last Gunfighter Standing*

*Sins of the Father*
*The Guns of Jacob Blade Vigilante*
*Vigilante Killer on the Run*
*The Crow's Shadow*

**Other Fiction**

*Angel on His Shoulder*
*She's No Angel*
*Child of the Flame*
*Pip's Revenge*
*Wallace in Underland*
*Further Adventures of Wallace in Underland*
*Dead Letter and Other Tales*
*The White Dragons*
*The Dragon's Lair*
*Dragon Slayer*
*The Last Gunfighters*
*The Culling*
*Frontier Justice: Bass Reeves, Deputy U.S. Marshal*
*Angel on His Shoulder – Revised Edition*
*Battle at the Galactic Junkyard*
*Mountain Man*
*Devil's Lake*
*Vixen*
*Awakening*
*Chase the Sun*
*The Lady's Last Song*
*Dead Letter and Other Tales – Revised Edition*
*Catch Me if You Can*
*A Cowboy's Christmas Carol*
*Hard Ride to Glenrose, Texas*
*Toby Giles: Tarnished Badge*
*Marshals of Dusty Saddle (short story anthology)*
*Sheriff B.J. Kincaid: Shoot Fast or Die*
*Guns Along Carson's Ford (with Fred Staff)*
*Sheriff B.J. Kincaid: Cry of the Raven*
*Breath of the Dragon*
*Sheriff B.J. Kincaid: Bullet for a Bad Man*
*Toby Giles: The Walls of Jericho*
*Tom Steele: A Day of Reckoning*
*Sheriff B.J. Kincaid: Showdown at High Noon*

*The Blazing Guns of the Lawman Kincaid*
*Toby Giles: One More River to Cross*
*Back to Bear Creek*
*The Calico Cowboy*
*Menace in the Mountain Mist*
*Snowbound*

## Nonfiction

*Things I Learned from My Grandmother About Leadership and Life*
*Taking Charge: Effective Leadership for the Twenty-First Century*
*Grab the Brass Ring*
*African Places*
*A Portrait of Africa*
*There's Always a Plan B*
*In the Line of Fire*
*Advice for the Insecure Writer*
*Looking at Life Through My Lens*
*Ethical Dilemmas and the Practice of Diplomacy*
*Making America Grate Again*
*DC Street Art*
*Things I Learned from My Grandmother, Second Edition*
*Feathers, Fur, and Flowers*
*Backyards and Byways*
*American Heroes*
*Invasion of the Swamp Creatures*
*Ethical Diplomacy and the Trump Administration*

## Children's Books

*The Yak and the Yeti*
*Samantha and the Bully*
*Molly Learns to Share*
*Where is Teddy?*
*Catie and Mister Hop-Hop*
*Tommy Learns to Count*
*Catie Goes to School*

*Caleb Johnson: Mountain Man: Snowbound*

## Writing as Ben Carter

*William Coburn: Cowboy vs the Sea Monster*

*Charles Ray*

## ABOUT THE AUTHOR

Charles Ray began writing fiction in his early teens, when he won a national Sunday school magazine short story competition, but, having been taught to read by his mother when he was four, and having read every gook in his school library by the time he reached fifth grade, he's been making up stories much longer. Painfully shy until mid-way through his freshman year in high school, writing was his primary form of communication—when he chose to communicate, preferring the company of books to people.

He joined the army in 1962, right out of high school, and during the next twenty years, along with soldiering, he moonlighted as a newspaper or magazine journalist, artist, and photographer in the U.S., and abroad. In the 1970s, he was the editorial cartoonist for the Spring Lake (NC) News, a small weekly, and did cartoons and art for a number of publications, including Ebony, Essence, Eagle and Swan and Buffalo (a now-defunct magazine that was dedicated to showcasing the contributions of African-Americans to American military history.

He retired from the army in 1982 and joined the U.S. Foreign Service, serving until he retired in 2012 as a diplomat in posts in Asia and Africa.

He's worked and traveled throughout the world (Antarctica is the only continent he's never visited), and now, as a full-time bohemian (a catch word for someone who engages in creative pursuits of all kinds), he continues to roam the globe looking for subjects to write about, photograph, or paint.

A native of East Texas, he now calls suburban Montgomery County, Maryland home.

For more information on his works, and other projects, check out one of the following sites:

http://charlesray-author.com/
http://charlesaray.blogspot.com
http://charlieray45.wordpress.com
http://www.twitter.com/charlieray45
http://www.flickr.com'charlesray45
http://www.viewbug.com/member/charlesray
https://fineartamerica.com/profiles/2-charles-ray.html

Authors write to be read, and that can only happen when readers are made aware of what they've written. Reviews are a great way to inform readers of new works, so if you've liked this book, please be so kind as to leave a short review on Amazon, Goodreads, or the site from which you purchased it.

Made in the USA
Monee, IL
29 January 2021